DATE DUE			
OCT 10			

The Reindeer People

written and illustrated by TED LEWIN

Macmillan Publishing Company   New York   Maxwell Macmillan Canada   Toronto

Maxwell Macmillan International   New York   Oxford   Singapore   Sydney

To the Sami people

Library of Congress Cataloging-in-Publication Data
Lewin, Ted. The reindeer people / written and illustrated by Ted Lewin. — 1st ed.   p.   cm.   Summary: Portrays the life of the Sami people in Lapland. ISBN 0-02-757390-7   1. Sami (European people)—Juvenile literature.   [1. Sami (European people)]   I. Title. DL42.L36R45   1994   948.97'7—dc20   93-19252

Lapland is a country without borders. It runs across the top of Norway, Sweden, Finland, and Russia, above the Arctic Circle. It is the land of the reindeer and of the reindeer people.

The origin of the Lapp people, or Sami, as they call themselves, remains a mystery, but they have hunted wild reindeer and fished in Lapland for centuries. From the eighteenth century on, they have herded reindeer. It is still their most important trade, and a way of life. The reindeer herds provide meat and milk, clothing, tools, a cash crop, and the raw material for domestic crafts, or *duodji.*

In the spring, the Sami follow their migrating herds from the winter grazing grounds to the coast where they will spend the summer.

Every Easter, Sami people from all over gather in the little municipality of Kautokeino in northern Norway for a great festival. They roar around on snowmobiles like knights on chargers, wearing white reindeer coats with multicolored ribbons fluttering from tall red hats. They marry in felt tunics of blue and red, ablaze with ornaments of silver and gold. They spill out their passions in *yoik,* their own special kind of song, and they have reindeer sledge races, their own special kind of madness.

THE SLEDGE RIDE

Snow is blowing in fierce blasts off the frozen river, and the sun is eye-shattering. Ola is going out to his camp to check on his herd. Like a cowboy, he bulldogs five half-wild reindeer into their harnesses and hitches them to the sledges, then rounds up three more for spares. He takes the lead reindeer by the harness and begins to run. The whole line jerks into motion, each reindeer startled as its line snaps tight. It's a leaping, grunting, bucking, eye-bulging, tongue-lolling stampede.

They jerk and leap out onto the frozen river, as wild as broncos. One gets its legs caught in the ropes and stumbles, antlers flailing. Another, refusing to pull, drops like a sack of cement and is dragged along on the hard snow by the others. They all grind to a halt. After Ola untangles them, he replaces the balky reindeer with one of the spares.

Ola again takes the lead reindeer by the halter and begins to trot, causing the whole chain reaction to start over. When Ola is satisfied with the pace, he drops down onto his sledge. The whole procession settles into a smooth rhythm, and the reindeer breathe easier.

For a while, the only sounds in the stillness of the frozen plain are the sliding and crunching of the plastic-covered runners through the snow. The trail becomes enclosed by some low birch trees, and something spooks the reindeer. They bound in different directions, then panic, each one trying to pass the one in front. One reindeer leaps over a sledge, tipping it over. The other sledges are pulled into deep snow, and the reindeer sink to their bellies. They grunt and strain in the harnesses, but they can't budge the bogged-down sledges and collapse in exhaustion. Ola stands off to the side calmly sorting things out in his mind.

Then, with great tugging, and a few well-placed kicks, they are back out on the hard snow trail at full gallop. Five more hours of this, and Ola's camp appears in the distance.

THE LAVU

Inside the herding tent, or *lavu*, at the camp, a fire tended by Ola's mother glows in a shallow pit. Green birch branches are spread on the ground with reindeer hides laid on top. Around the fire pit, the lichens and grasses of summer are exposed. A cold light plays in the dark, smoky interior through the open top of the lavu.

There is a big black kettle, a very black coffeepot, and an ancient red-and-blue painted wooden box with rounded corners. In front of the tent, Ola cuts kindling with a razor-sharp ax.

As the piece of sky at the open top of the lavu turns from light to dark, the temperature outside drops to thirty degrees below zero. Inside by the fire, it is thirty-two degrees above.

Ola's mother hangs a big pot of reindeer stew, called *bidus*, over the fire. Later she sets the coffeepot on the embers. In the distance, reindeer bells clank and a fox barks.

Stepping out into the frigid Arctic night to cut another tree for the fire, Ola looks up at the indigo sky. Directly overhead is a brilliant arch of eerie greenish light: the northern lights. It covers the entire dome of the sky. The light moves back and forth in a fine veil, finally gathering at the top in a glowing mass. An orange, full moon has just managed to clear the horizon and lingers as if frozen there. Standing on the hard snow at minus thirty degrees, wearing reindeer-skin boots stuffed with dry grass, Ola's feet are warm and dry.

The snow gets softer near the trees, and Ola sinks waist-deep. He cuts a tree at the snow line, but in spring, the cut will be in the middle of the trunk.

THE HERD

The sky is salmon pink, and the sun very near setting. There is a snow haze, and the snow on the ground looks light blue. Grazing in a hollow is the herd, four hundred strong. Nearby, Ola "sits" his snowmobile as a cowboy "sits" his horse. He starts it up and moves in to round up the herd. The herd begins to circle, then breaks into a gallop, bells clanking. The snow flies as they race past like a living cave painting.

In the tightly packed herd, three big males stand together, their antlers blending into an incredible piece of Arctic sculpture.

Ola lounges on the seat of his snowmobile, deftly rolling a cigarette, as comfortable and content as his reindeer at fifteen degrees below zero.

THE CORRAL

On a distant frozen hillside, the wind blows with a knife edge. Two huge men and an old woman with a face like leather and a bright red hat are bringing in a herd of reindeer for the winter market.

The woman opens the gate as the two men bring big bags of feed, hay, and soft green lichen into the yard. The reindeer pour into the enclosure like a flood. The low sun strikes their antlers with golden light, and they glow against the blue snow hills.

Once inside the corral, they wheel around like a school of fish, first to the left. The men inside wave their arms, and the reindeer turn and swirl to the right.

One of the big men throws his lariat into the mass of running animals. He catches one from someone else's herd and pulls on the green nylon line until the bucking animal is reeled in. Both men take him by the antlers and wrestle him to the corral gate where he's set free. He leaps into the air and is momentarily framed by the sun, shining yellow through a section of cloth fence. He trots away, free, but goes nowhere. He could go on to Siberia but stops in the yard as if lost, reluctant to leave the herd.

They lasso several others and release them. The herd wheels this way and that, wild and skittish, finally settling down to feed. Their silhouettes, and those of the men working, play on the back of the sunlit cloth fence like shadow puppets.

THE RACE

The reindeer are tied to clumps of birch trees near their sledges. Fur-clad men with lariats encircling their bodies like bandoliers move among them. They work and re-work the harnesses with bare hands and sharp knives, their mittens always on the snow just in front of them. Families sit on their snow-mobiles or in sledge carriages with reindeer-skin covers—an Arctic picnic.

A crowd begins to gather as a reindeer is tugged by a long rope and halter to the starting line. His eyes bulge, and his front legs are splayed and stiff. Two men approach warily, then quickly grab him in a headlock. He bucks wildly, and they hold the struggling creature for dear life as they slip on the harness.

The driver, his number tied to his chest, reins in hand, waits at the ready.

The men let the reindeer go, and he explodes toward the track. The driver leaps onto the sledge in the nick of time, and they disappear down the chute of saplings and around the bend. The course is one kilometer long. They come down the straightaway in a flash, the reindeer running his splaylegged gait at full tilt, his eyes bulging, his tongue lolling (his only way to cool off).

He passes the finish line without breaking stride and keeps going. The crowd scatters.

Neither the sledge nor the reindeer has brakes, so in order to stop, the driver falls off holding on to the reins and slides facedown in the snow, while the reindeer runs into the crowd until he's subdued by three or four men. One of the men, with two knives swinging on his belt, yoiks, and the wonderful sound of it is like the race itself, wild and crazy and hair-raising.

Another reindeer is soon tugged out to the starting line, and the whole thing begins again.

THE WEDDING

Beyond the gaily painted doors the church interior glows with the soft golden light of chandeliers. The pews are packed with people— waves of high red hats and ribbons.

The bride is sheathed in gold and silver. The crowd surges forward to take pictures. They carry video cameras and wear reindeer clothes. When the bride and groom proceed down the aisle, red and blue rick-rack and gold and silver blur and gleam. Knife sheaths made of reindeer antlers swing from wide, low-slung, silver-studded belts.

The bride and groom come through the inner church doors into the dark foyer, followed by the crowd. As everyone spills outside, cold white daylight sculpts their faces.

Outside, the entire wedding party, bride and groom in the center, arrange themselves into a living fairy tale. One by one, people come up to shake hands. The women wear gorgeous fringed shawls over their red-and-blue tunics. They all wear reindeer-skin boots curled up at the toes, and high red hats with long ribbons fluttering in the cold Arctic breeze. Finally, the last hands are shaken, and the couple walks arm in arm out of the fairy tale into a waiting taxi and the twentieth century.